Dear mouse friends,
Welcome to the world of

Geronimo Stilton

The Editorial Staff of
The Rodent's Gazette

1. Linda Thinslice
2. Sweetie Cheesetriangle
3. Ratella Redfur
4. Soya Mousehao
5. Cheesita de la Pampa
6. Mouseanna Mousetti
7. Yale Youngmouse
8. Toni Tinypaw
9. Tina Spicytail
10. William Shortpaws
11. Valerie Vole
12. Trap Stilton
13. Branwen Musclemouse
14. Zeppola Zap
15. Merenguita Gingermouse
16. Ratsy O'Shea
17. Rodentrick Roundrat
18. Teddy von Muffler
19. Thea Stilton
20. Erronea Misprint
21. Pinky Pick
22. Ya-ya O'Cheddar
23. Mousella MacMouser
24. Kreamy O'Cheddar
25. Blasco Tabasco
26. Toffie Sugarsweet
27. Tylerat Truemouse
28. Larry Keys
29. Michael Mouse
30. Geronimo Stilton
31. Benjamin Stilton
32. Briette Finerat
33. Raclette Finerat

Geronimo Stilton
A learned and brainy
mouse; editor of
The Rodent's Gazette

Thea Stilton
Geronimo's sister and
special correspondent at
The Rodent's Gazette

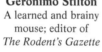
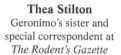

Trap Stilton
An awful joker;
Geronimo's cousin and
owner of the store
Cheap Junk for Less

Benjamin Stilton
A sweet and loving
nine-year-old mouse;
Geronimo's favorite
nephew

Geronimo Stilton

A FABUMOUSE VACATION FOR GERONIMO

Scholastic Inc.

New York   Toronto   London   Auckland   Sydney
Mexico City   New Delhi   Hong Kong   Buenos Aires

ISBN 978-0-439-55971-3

Based on an original idea by Elisabetta Dami.

www.geronimostilton.com

Published by Scholastic Inc., 557 Broadway, New York, NY 10012. SCHOLASTIC and associated logos are trademarks and/or registered trademarks of Scholastic Inc.

Stilton is the name of a famous English cheese. It is a registered trademark of the Stilton Cheese Makers' Association. For more information, go to www.stiltoncheese.com.

Text by Geronimo Stilton
Original title *Quella stratopica vacanza alla pensione Mirasorci...*
Cover by Larry Keys
Illustrations by Larry Keys
Graphics by Merenguita Gingermouse

Special thanks to Kathryn Cristaldi
Interior design by Kay Petronio

20 19 18 17 16   11 12 13 14 15 16/0

Printed in the U.S.A.   40
First printing, July 2004

THE NAME IS STILTON, GERONIMO STILTON . . .

One morning, I woke up sweating like a mouse in a cat parade. August is always hot in New Mouse City. But this year was the worst. The air was so *HEAVY*, it was hard to breathe. And the sun was scorching. It made my fur feel like it was on fire.

Cheese niblets! I couldn't wait for my vacation. . . .

I turned the shower on ice-cold. Then I

jumped in. Ah! There's nothing like a cold shower on a hot summer day. I began to sing one of my favorite tunes.

"If you're happy and you know it, clap your paws!"

After my shower, I decided to make myself a whisker-licking-good breakfast. I trotted toward my MEGAHUGE FRIDGE. It was filled with lots of yummy foods — cheese, cheese, and more cheese!

Should I chomp on a cheddar biscuit? Or spread some jam on a slice of SWISS? At last, I settled on a vitamin-packed mozzarella milk shake. It was delicious. I patted my tummy. What a perfect way to start my day.

I left my mouse hole and headed for my office. *Maybe the heat won't be so bad today,* I thought.

I settled on a vitamin-packed mozzarella milk shake.

I was wrong. The ground was so hot, smoke rose from my paws. The air was so stuffy, I felt **FAINT**.

Cheese niblets! I couldn't wait for my vacation. . . .

I decided to take the subway. The train was about to leave. I jumped on just before the doors slammed shut. Phew! One second later and I would have lost my tail! I plopped down into an empty seat. At that

moment, I realized the mouse sitting next to me was a rodent I knew very well. It was **Pinky Pick**. Do you know her? She's my very young assistant editor.

Oh, how rude. I completely forgot to introduce myself. My name is Stilton, *Geronimo Stilton*. I am an author and a publisher. I run the most popular newspaper here on Mouse Island. It's called *The Rodent's Gazette*.

I KNOW A SONG . . .

As soon as she saw me, Pinky grinned. Then she began to sing in a high-pitched squeak.

"I KNOW A SONG
THAT DRIVES MICE WILD,
BUT I DON'T CARE 'CAUSE
IT MAKES ME SMILE!
YEAH, YEAH, YEAH . . ."

Her squeak got louder and louder. It sounded like CAT claws on a chalkboard. I shot her a murderous look. But she just kept on squeaking. One thing you should know about Pinky, she loves to get under my fur.

"I KNOW A SONG THAT DRIVES MICE WILD,
BUT I DON'T CARE 'CAUSE IT MAKES ME SMILE! ♫♫♫
YEAH, YEAH, YEAH, YEAH, YEAH, YEAH, YEAH ...
I KNOW A SONG THAT DRIVES MICE WILD, ♪
BUT I DON'T CARE 'CAUSE IT MAKES ME SMILE!
YEAH, YEAH, YEAH, YEAH, YEAH, YEAH, YEAH ..."

Pinky's screech filled the subway car. By now, every rodent was staring at us. Well, they were doing more than just staring. They were **GLARING**! I gulped. The crowd was getting ugly. Some gnashed their teeth. Others stamped their paws. They looked like they wanted to put a muzzle on little Pinky.

"**PUT A LID ON IT!**" one mouse demanded.

"Stuff a sock in it!" another added.

Just then, a lady mouse wagged a paw in my face.

"What kind of a father are you?" she scolded. "Tell your daughter to stop that AWFUL SQUEAKING!"

I chewed my whiskers.

"But, um, see, she isn't my daughter," I tried to explain.

Suddenly, Pinky broke into a crazy dance number. She whirled and twirled around me. Her ear-piercing squeak was enough to make a grown mouse cry. "What do you think, Daddy dearest, Popsy Wopsy," she SHRIEKED. "Do I sound like one of the Three Squeaks?" Pinky loved the Three Squeaks. They were the hottest female mouse band on Mouse Island.

"I KNOW A SONG THAT
DRIVES MICE WILD,

BUT I DON'T CARE
'CAUSE IT MAKES ME SMILE!

YEAH, YEAH, YEAH,
YEAH, YEAH, YEAH, YEAH . . .

I KNOW A SONG THAT
DRIVES MICE WILD,

BUT I DON'T CARE
'CAUSE IT MAKES ME SMILE!

YEAH, YEAH, YEAH,
YEAH, YEAH, YEAH, YEAH . . ."

The lady mouse shot me a dirty look. "Popsy Wopsy," I heard her mutter.

Pinky winked at me. She kept singing at the top of her lungs. I closed my eyes. I pictured myself firing Pinky. STILTON FIRES SINGING MOUSE! the headline would read. No, I couldn't do it. You can't fire a mouse for singing.

Angry voices interrupted my thoughts.

"*MAKE HER STOP!*" a rodent cried.

"**Enough already!**" called another.

"For heaven's sake!"

"I CAN'T STAND IT ANYMORE!"

"SQUEEEAK!!"

Luckily, we had reached our stop. I grabbed Pinky by a paw and scampered off the train. I had never been so humiliated in my life.

Cheese niblets! I couldn't wait for my vacation. . . .

I had never been so humiliated in my life.

WHAT A HEAT WAVE!

When we reached the office, Pinky took off. "Catch you later, Popsicle!" she **CALLED OUT** before she disappeared.

I hung my head. What did I do to deserve that mouse? She was so irritating. She was so obnoxious. She could drive a perfectly normal rodent to eat rat poison!

Of course, you are probably wondering why I put up with Pinky. After all, I am her boss. But there is one thing I didn't tell you about Pinky. She is a **genius**. Yes, an honest-to-goodmouse **genius**! Last year, Pinky came

Swisssshhhhhhh...

up with an idea for a magazine for young mice. She called it **Fur Kids Only**. Now it is the most popular magazine for mouslets in New Mouse City. Pinky's just a teenager, but she's one of the brainiest rodents I know!

After Pinky left, I pushed open the door to my office. What a heat wave! I could hardly breathe. Even my whiskers were sweating. I turned the dial on the AIR CONDITIONER. But it must have gotten stuck. A blast of icy air hit me in the snout.

Within minutes, I was freezing my tail off.

The wall thermometer read thirty degrees below zero! It was colder than the time I tried skiing on the slopes of Ratrun Mountain. At least then, I was able to take breaks at the Cozytail Lodge.

My secretary, Mousella, found me shivering in a corner of the room. She shook her head. "Mr. Stilton, you'll catch your death in here," she scolded.

I switched off the air conditioner. *I wasn't about to freeze to death right before my vacation.* Five minutes later, it was boiling again. The HEAT melted the icicles on my whiskers. I groaned. My good silk tie was soaked.

I was a mess. Upset, I called the air-conditioner rat. "There must be something wrong with this machine," I explained.

"What's the problem?" he smirked. "If

you're hot, you switch it on. If you're cold, just switch it off!"

I chewed my whiskers to keep from screaming.

Cheese niblets! I couldn't wait for my vacation. . . .

I switched on an old copper fan my grandfather **WILLIAM SHORTPAWS** had hung from the ceiling. Grandfather was the founder of *The Rodent's Gazette.* Years ago, he ran the business with an iron paw. He was known for being the cheapest mouse in the pack, which is why he was nicknamed **CHEAP MOUSE WILLY**!
He only brushed his teeth once a

Founder of
The Rodent's Gazette

My grandfather **WILLIAM SHORTPAWS**, *also known as* **CHEAP MOUSE WILLY**

week to save money on toothpaste.

As soon as I switched on the fan, papers began to fly all over the place.

"Mousella! *HEEEELP!*" I squeaked in a panic.

My secretary ran into the office. Paper rained down like giant snowflakes. Mousella shook her head. "How did you manage to make such a **MESS**?"

she yelled. But she helped me put the place back in order.

By now, I was really sweating. It was hotter than the kitchen of the Greasy Rat Café in the summertime. *Cheese niblets! I couldn't wait for my vacation.*

Just then, I remembered something. My grandfather always kept a small personal-sized fan in the cellar. I raced down to find it. Back in my office, I set it up away from the papers on my desk. Then I switched it on. **AH, RELIEF!**

I was as **cool** as a cheddar cheese log in my megahuge fridge!

I'm Too Fond of My Tail!

I had just started working when my door flew open. **Pinky Pick** skipped in. "Hi, Popsy Wopsy!" she squeaked with a grin. Then she plopped down on the edge of my desk.

That's it, I decided. I had to let Pinky know who was boss. I had to let her know I was running this mouse show. I jumped to my paws. *"DON'T CALL ME POPSY WOPSY!"* I shrieked. I thumped my tail on the floor angrily.

THUMP! THUMP . . . OUCH!

Oops. I had forgotten about the fan. My poor tail was getting sliced up by the blades! *"HELP!"* I cried. **I'm too fond of my tail!**

Mousella came running in. "What happened? What have you done now, Mr.

Stilton?" my secretary groaned.

Mousella drove me to the EMERGENCY ROOM at Mouse General. It was hard to get in the car with a fan attached to my tail. But I did it. An hour later, I was back in the office. My tail was all bandaged up. It looked like a mummy. A long, skinny snake mummy, that is.

Cheese niblets! I couldn't wait for my vacation....

AFTER ALL, WHO'S TO KNOW?

I was E X H A U S T E D. And it wasn't even lunchtime yet!

My tail was throbbing. I was behind with my work. And I was hotter than a pot of boiling cheese fondue!

I wiped the sweat from my whiskers. I had

my yellow underpants

to do something or I'd die of heatstroke. Well, OK, I wouldn't actually die, but you get the picture. I was desperate. I stripped down to my underwear. *After all*, I told myself, *who's to know?*

Then I pulled a black fan from my desk drawer. It was dotted with red satin hearts.

My aunt Sweetfur had left it in my office the last time she came to visit. Of course, normally I wouldn't be caught dead holding that silly fan. But, as I said, I was desperate.

Aunt Sweetfur's fan

Next, I got some ice cubes from the freezer. I wrapped them up in a pawkerchief. Then I wore it on my head to cool myself down. **After all**, I encouraged myself, **who's to know?**

I was feeling a little better. I stared out the window. The sun was blinding. I needed a pair of sunglasses.

my ice-cube pawkerchief

I dug through my desk drawer. I found a pair

Thea's rhinestone-studded purple sunglasses

of sunglasses. Too bad they belonged to my sister, Thea. They were bright purple and studded with rhinestones. Only my sister could wear something so tacky and still look good. **Ah, well**, I thought as I put them on. **Who's to know?**

My tail was still throbbing, so I put my paws up on my desk. Right then, **a pesky mosquito flew up my nostril**. That bug was buzzing around like he had just drunk ten cups of coffee. I know it's rude, but what could I do? I stuck my pawnail in my nose. **After all**, I comforted myself, **who's to know?**

At that very moment, the door creaked open....

At that very moment, the door creaked open. . . .

SHAME ON YOU, MR. STILTON!

In came *Sir Ratley von Snotfur* III. Who is Sir Ratley? He's the president of the CSA. The CSA is the most exclusive club in town. THE "C" STANDS FOR CENTRAL. THE "S" STANDS FOR SNOB. AND THE "A" STANDS FOR ACADEMY.

Sir Ratley took one look at me and choked. I tried to throw my clothes on, but it was too late. I was caught like a mouse in a trap. **WHAT** was I thinking? **WHAT** was I doing? **WHAT** happened to the sign on my door, PLEASE KNOCK BEFORE ENTERING?

Sir Ratley glanced at my underwear. Then he took in my sunglasses. Then he checked out the pawkerchief wrapped around my head. Last but not least, he stared at my pawnail up my nose.

"Mr. Stilton!" he thundered. "You are a disgrace!"

He showed me a gold medal and a formal letter. "Mr. Stilton, I came to present you with this medal," he sniffed. "You have been chosen MOST POLISHED MOUSE OF THE YEAR."

I jumped to my paws. This was the most exciting thing that ever happened to me! I had been dreaming of getting this award for ages.

"I'd like to thank the

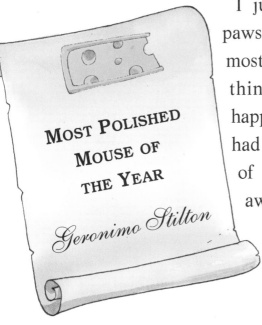

MOST POLISHED MOUSE OF THE YEAR

Geronimo Stilton

Academy for this award," I began. But before I could finish my speech, Sir Ratley interrupted me. He *ripped* the medal from my paws. *Now, that wasn't very polite,* I thought.

"After what I saw today, you can kiss this medal good-bye, Stilton!" he shrieked. "You are the most unpolished mouse I have ever seen!" His whiskers shook with disgust.

"B-B-But sir, you

s-s-see, um, I m-m-mean, actually . . ." I stuttered. I WAS SO EMBARRASSED, EVEN MY FUR WAS BLUSHING.

But Sir Ratley didn't seem to notice. He didn't care about my excuses. He had made up his mind. With one final sniff, he marched out of my office. "Shame on you, Mr. Stilton!" he squeaked. Then he slammed the door in my snout.

I was **CRUSHED**. I took off my glasses so I could cry freely.

Cheese niblets! I couldn't wait for my vacation. . . .

MIND YOUR EARS, STILTON!

I put my clothes back on. I couldn't stop sobbing. I was like a baby mouse on his first visit to the pediatrician. Just then, Pinky sailed through the door.

"I KNOW A SONG

♫ THAT DRIVES MICE WILD,

YEAH, YEAH, YEAH...

YEAH, YEAH, YEAH..."

she sang in her high-pitched squeak.

I groaned. Talk about kicking a mouse when he's down. That silly song was about to drive this mouse up the wall.

Pinky plopped down in a chair and rested her paws on my desk. "Check it out, Popsy Wopsy," she remarked, tossing the latest copy of **Fur Kids Only** at me. It had a special section filled with fun games to play on vacation.

I leafed through the magazine. "Hmm . . . very nice!" I admitted. As I said, Pinky can

Daddy dearest
Ratty Daddy
Popsy Wopsy

be annoying, but she is clever. Very clever indeed.

"By the way, Ratty Daddy, I'm leaving on vacation next week," she announced. "Don't miss me too much!"

I rolled my eyes. "I'll live," I told her. *Plus, I was off on my own vacation the next day.* Cheesecake! I couldn't wait to be off. I couldn't deal with the **HEAT**. I couldn't deal with the piles of work. And mostly I couldn't deal with Pinky Pick anymore!

Just then, the phone **rang**. I stretched out my paw to answer, but Pinky beat me to it.

"Hello, you've reached Mr. Stilton's office. This is his assistant **Pinky Pick** speaking," she squeaked. "Oh, hello, Mr. Crunchrat. What? You're going to buy one million copies of **Fur Kids Only** to give away with your Crunchrat Cheesy Chips? Wow! What fabumouse news!"she shrieked.

I grabbed the receiver. "Hello, Stilton speaking," I began.

But Crunchrat cut me short. He wanted to talk about Pinky Pick. He told me that she was the most brilliant mouse on my staff. He told me that I was lucky to have her. Then he went on about the latest copy of **Fur Kids Only**. He loved the special insert, **BLAH, BLAH, BLAH**. Pinky skipped out of the room, twirling her tail. Meanwhile, Crunchrat's voice droned on and on in my ear. I was glad he loved the magazine. But he never stopped squeaking. And I was getting tired.

So tired. Maybe it was the heat. Or maybe I just didn't want to hear any more about Pinky Pick. I put my head down on my desk. *I'll take a quick mouse nap,* I told myself. Within minutes, I was snoring. I dreamed I was vacationing on the SWISS CHEESE ISLANDS. Ah, the cool breeze off the ocean tickled my whiskers. The sand squished beneath my paws. But what was that sound? It was like a siren. Just like the wail of a police car. I woke up. I was wrong. It wasn't a police car. It was Crunchrat. He was wailing in my ear.

"Are you listening, Stilton?!" he bellowed. "I want you to give Ms. Pick a bonus or I will not buy a single copy of that magazine of yours! **DO YOU UNDERSTAND? DO YOU? DO YOU?**"

I snapped to attention. "Give Pinky a bonus!" I cried. "But I'm already paying her a ton!"

Just then, Pinky sailed back into the room. She was waving an advertisement for Crunchrat Cheesy Chips. It showed a picture of Crunchrat. He was ENORMOUSE! He was as big as my wardrobe! And he looked just like one of those sumo rat wrestlers.

Crunchrat continued to shriek in my ear. "I'm telling you, Stilton, if you don't do as I say, you'll be sorry!" he warned. "I'll twist your tail up in **knots**! I'll pull out all of your **fur**! I'll send your suit to the **dry cleaners** with you in it! I'll —"

I quickly cut him off. "Don't worry, Mr.

Crunchrat," I choked. "Consider it done. I'll give Pinky that bonus right away."

After all, I wasn't a cheesebrain. I wasn't about to lose my fur for Pinky Pick.

When I hung up the phone, Pinky stretched out her paw. "You can pay me now, Popsy Wopsy," she smirked. "I could use the extra dough on my vacation. Ten percent should do it. No, on second thought, better make it fifty percent."

I grabbed my checkbook. Tears poured from my eyes. Who would think such a little mouse could cost me such a big fortune? *Cheese niblets! I couldn't wait for my vacation....*

AH, THE SEA . . .

As soon as Pinky left, I called my travel agency, **THE WANDER RAT**. Ms. Samantha Sweetpaws answered the phone.

"Mr. Stilton," she cooed. "I'm sending you to the most *fabumouse* place! It's

SAMANTHA SWEETPAWS

called Happy Tail Island. It's one of the Hamster Islands—far, far away from civilization. You'll be on a beautiful private beach. The water is CRYSTAL CLEAR. The coral reef is teeming with fish. And the view is spectacular. You leave tomorrow at seven A.M. sharp!"

I clapped my paws. The place sounded perfect. A quiet beach all to myself! I couldn't wait to leave. I'd had enough of this rat race.

That evening, I packed my suitcase. I put in a swimsuit, flippers, goggles, sunglasses, and suntan lotion. I would take my laptop, too, so I could write in peace. And, of course, I would bring lots and lots of books.

There's nothing like the sea!

I love to read on vacation.

As I packed, I began to sing.

"AH, THE SEA,

THERE'S NOTHING

LIKE THE SEA. . . ."

FURDRICK FIXIT'S SECRET

At two o'clock in the morning, the phone **rang**. I was still half asleep. "Stilson, speaking, *Geronimouse Stilson*," I managed to mumble.

It was **Preston Pressmouse**, the printer. "Mr. Stilton! The press has broken down! We can't print anymore!" he shrieked in my ear. "*The Rodent's Gazette* won't be ready for tomorrow!"

I jumped out of bed. Now I was wide awake. What a nightmare! If the paper didn't come out, rodents might decide to read

Preston Pressmouse

another paper. They might like it better than *The Rodent's Gazette.* *The Gazette* would be **DOOMED**! I couldn't let that happen.

I ran breathlessly to the pressroom. Rancid rat hairs! Preston was right. The machines were totally jammed!

I **called** the technician, *TERRY TECHRAT*, but he was busy working on another broken printing press.

I **called** his partner, but he was away on vacation.

TERRY TECHRAT

I **called** the butcher, the baker, and the candlestick maker. But no one was home. Doesn't any mouse believe in a good night's sleep anymore?

I left the pressroom feeling beat. I decided to take the elevator to my office to think. I sat behind my desk, staring into space. My gaze fell on a stone sculpture of my grandfather WILLIAM SHORTPAWS, aka CHEAP MOUSE WILLY. He started the paper in his garage so many years ago. He had worked long and hard to make *The Rodent's Gazette* a success. I couldn't let him down now. But what could I do? I had to find some mouse who could fix a broken printing press.

GRANDFATHER WILLIAM SHORTPAWS

Founder of
The Rodent's Gazette

The Rodent's Gazette

1. Main Entrance
2. Printing presses (books and newspapers are printed here)
3. Accounts department
4. Editorial room (where the editors, illustrators, and designers work)
5. Geronimo Stilton's office
6. Storage space for Geronimo's books

Just then, I had an **IDEA**. I remembered an old printing technician from my grandfather's time. He had retired several years ago. His name was FURDRICK FIXIT. He was an incredibly sweet old mouse. Always squeaking a happy tune while he worked. Always lending a helping paw. I sent him a special cheese-scented holiday card every year. And now and then, I would give him a call to squeak about the old days.

Now I called him in a panic. I told him about the broken printing press. "Could you come and look at it?" I begged Furdrick. "You are my last hope!"

FURDRICK FIXIT

Five minutes later, Furdrick arrived. He practically skipped into the PRESSROOM. I could tell he was thrilled to be there. After all, he had worked at *The Rodent's Gazette* for forty years. It was like his second home.

He stooped over the broken machine. He tapped his cane on one side of the press, then the other.

"Ah, yes, the old RAT-PRINT 500," he announced. "This is the same machine I printed on years ago! I remember it well!"

I nodded. "That's right, Furdrick," I agreed. "It is the same old press. Can you fix it?"

Furdrick threw me a sly grin. "Does a mouse eat cHeeSe on Thanksgiving?" he asked.

I figured that meant yes. The old mouse put his paw around my shoulder. "My dear Geronimo," he began, "I know a trick to get this thing working again. But it's a secret. You must not tell a single rodent. I'm only telling you because you are William Shortpaws's grandson."

I nodded. *What could be so secret about an old printing press?* I wondered.

Furdrick showed me a spot under the control panel. It looked like a small dent.

"See this mark?" he said in a low voice. "It was made by your grandfather's paw. One day, a book printed upside down. William was furious. He kicked the press. From then on, whenever the machine got too hot, it stopped printing. Just like now."

Furdrick snickered. "That grandfather of yours has a bit of a temper," he added.

I shook my head. Grandfather has more than a bit of a temper. He has a **humongous temper**! When I was a young mouse, I was always tripping over my tail. One time, I accidentally knocked over a bookcase at Grandfather William's house. He threw a fit. To this day, I'm still not allowed to set paw in his library.

Grandfather William kicked the printing press.

Then there was the time I squashed all of the flowers in his garden. Grandfather put up a gate just to keep me out. And who could forget the time I knocked over that bowl of steaming-hot cheese soup?

Furdrick's voice interrupted my thoughts. "So do you want to know how to FIX this

BAMBAMBAMBAMBAMB

thing?" he asked, grinning. I opened my mouth to squeak but never had a chance. Before I could stop him, Furdrick began running toward the printing press. Then he gave it a good swift kick.

Bam-bam-bam! Bam-bam-bam!
Bam-bam-bam!

BAMBAMBAMBAMBAM

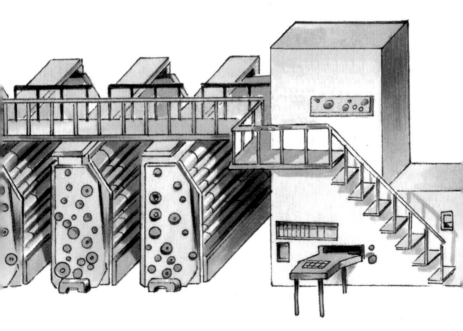

There was a series of loud thumps—and then the printer began churning out paper. It worked! Copies of *The Rodent's Gazette* spilled out of the machine.

I was full of admiration. "Thanks, Furdrick!" I squeaked happily.

Furdrick smiled. I could tell he was proud of himself. "Guess this old mouse still has the *touch*!" he chuckled. Then he jumped on his bicycle and pedaled off.

INK...

AH, THE
MOUNTAINS . . .

I went back home, *exhausted*. It was already morning. I hadn't slept a wink. I crawled under my covers. *Maybe I'll go to work late,* I thought. Or I could just take the whole day off. Yes, that sounded like a good plan. Every mouse deserves a little vacation now and then.

Suddenly, my eyes popped open. "Vacation!" I shrieked. Holey cheese! Today was the first day of my vacation! I glanced at my clock. It was seven-fifteen. I'd missed my plane to Happy Tail Island!

I called the travel agency. Unfortunately, there were no other flights leaving for the island. But Ms. Sweetpaws cheered me up.

"Don't worry, Mr. Stilton," she squeaked. "I have another vacation spot you may enjoy. It's a comfortable chalet on Coldcreeps Peak. LOTS OF BEAUTIFUL SNOWCAPPED MOUNTAINS, UNSPOILED NATURE . . ."

I told her it sounded wonderful. I just *had* to get out of the city.

Ms. Sweetpaws booked my trip. "Now, please pay attention, Mr. Stilton," she advised. "You leave tomorrow morning at nine o'clock."

That evening, I unpacked my suitcase. I took out the swimsuit, the goggles, and the flippers. I put in a pair of hiking boots, a woolen tail warmer, and my warmest coat.

As I packed, I began to sing.

"AH, THE MOUNTAINS, THERE'S NOTHING LIKE THE MOUNTAINS. . . ."

There's nothing like the mountains!

WATER UNDER THE BOOKS

At eleven o'clock that evening, the phone rang. It was the paper's storemouse, **PACKRAT PETE.**

"Mr. Stilton!" he screamed in my ear. "A bus crashed into the hydrant right in front of The Rodent's Gazette Building. Our warehouse is *FLOODED*. All the books are getting soaked. It's an absolute disaster!"

I couldn't believe it. My luck was worse than a mouse who's been cornered by a black cat! I raced to the warehouse in a panic. The water was pouring in so fast, even a sewer rat would have trouble riding the waves.

PACKRAT PETE

"Quick! We have to move the books somewhere dry!" I shouted to the workmice.

I put on a pair of blue overalls. Then I raced next door to TUTTI FRUTTI. It's a shop that sells cheese-flavored ice cream, owned by my good friend LICKETY SPLITZ. Lickety lives in a one-bedroom hole right above his shop. He likes to be close to his ice cream. He also likes to eat it. Lickety has a big, round belly. He says his belly is a free advertisement for his delicious ice creams. Have you ever tasted cHeeSe-FLaVored ice creaM? It's one of my favorite treats.

But I didn't have time to think about ice cream now. I had work to do. Lickety said it was okay to store the books in his place. We worked through the night, moving box after box. At last, we were done.

"Thank you, Lickety," I said. "You are a **true friend**."

Lickety waved his paw. "Don't mention it," he squeaked. Then he gave me a free double-scoop ice cream cone. It was **extra-sharp cheddar** with a cherry on top. Yum! My favorite! Normally, I don't eat ice cream cones for breakfast. But this was a special treat. Plus, it was the first day of my vacation.

Suddenly, I jumped to my paws. "My vacation!" I cried. I glanced at my watch. It was already ten o'clock. "**CHeeSe NibLetS!** I've missed my plane again!"

I raced to the travel agency.

LICKETY SPLITZ

AH, ADVENTURE . . .

Ms. Sweetpaws sighed when she heard my story. "Mr. Stilton, how about a fascinating trip to the Fossil Forest?" she suggested. "It's on the slopes of the volcano Gong-gong-bang-a-gong-dong. It will be quite an adventure. Departure is tomorrow at noon."

I accepted. I unpacked my suitcase. Then I put in my camera, a pair of jungle boots, a sun helmet, and a mosquito net.

As I packed, I began to sing.

"AH, ADVENTURE. THERE'S NOTHING LIKE ADVENTURE. . . ."

There's nothing like adventure. . . .

I WOULD DO
ANYTHING FOR YOU . . .

Next morning, just as I was leaving for the airport, the phone rang.

An excited voice squeaked, "Geronimooo!"

It was my Aunt Sweetfur. She lived in a mouse hole a few blocks away. She was always forgetting things like her glasses and her cell phone and her fur brush. But she never forgot my birthday. She was my favorite aunt.

"Heeeelp! Help me, Geronimo!" Aunt Sweetfur was shrieking. "My mouse hole is on FIRE!"

My whiskers stood on end. "Hold tight, Auntie!" I ordered. "I'm on my way!"

I called the fire department. Then I raced to Aunt Sweetfur's place. The fire department

I picked her up . . . and raced down the stairs.

wasn't there yet. What could I do? I was afraid of fire. But I had to be brave. I raced up the wooden staircase, which was already beginning to burn.

I spotted Aunt Sweetfur through the thick smoke. "I'm here, Auntie!" I cried. I picked her up. Then I raced back down the stairs. A beam fell from the ceiling, sending sparks flying. **BURNING** embers grazed my tail.

I came out panting. Luckily, Aunt Sweetfur was fine.

"Thank you, my darling nephew," she said with a sigh. "You're always there for me when I need you."

I smiled. "For you, Auntie, I'd do anything!" I squeaked. And I meant it. After all, I had just walked through fire for her!

I headed home. I was in no rush this time. I had already missed my plane . . . again.

AH, ART . . .

A few minutes later, my cell phone rang.

It was Ms. Sweetpaws. "Mr. Stilton?" she squeaked. "Why haven't you left yet?"

I chewed my whiskers. "Um, well, um, I sort of missed the plane," I stammered. "But it wasn't my fault. . . ."

Ms. Sweetpaws snorted. Then I heard her shuffling some papers. "Well, I can send you on a cruise. You'll travel all the way to Egypt. You can visit the pyramids. And lots of other wonderful Egyptian monuments," she offered.

I accepted right away. This vacation sounded fabumouse.

"Just remember, Mr. Stilton," Ms. Sweetpaws warned. "Your plane leaves tomorrow

evening at eight o'clock sharp!"

That night, I unpacked my suitcase once more. This time, I took a swimsuit, shorts, a pair of binoculars, a notebook, my camera, and *A Field Mouse's Guide to Egypt*.

As I packed, I began to sing.

"AH, ART, THERE'S NOTHING LIKE ART. . . ."

There's nothing like art. . . .

FRIED MUSSELS WITH EXTRA-HOT CHILI

That evening, I got a call from my cousin Trap. He invited me to dinner. Trap once had a job as a cook in a spooky castle in **TRANSRATANIA**. Now he thinks he's a master chef. To tell the truth, Trap's cooking is nothing to squeak home about. But my cousin is so conceited. He thinks he could have his own cooking show on Mouse TV!

When I got to Trap's place, he was busy at the stove. A cloud of smoke hung over his head.

"Cousinkins, you're in for a real treat!" he grinned. "For starters, I've made yummy **fried mussels**!"

I chewed my whiskers. You see, sometimes

shellfish upsets my stomach. "F-F-F-Fried m-mussels," I stammered. "Are they f-f-fresh?"

Trap just shook his head. Then he filled my plate. "Germeister, you are such a 'fraidy mouse," he smirked. "Of course these mussels are fresh. Take a nibble."

After the fried mussels, Trap brought out some clam soup. It reeked of **GARLIC**. I choked down a few spoonfuls.

Next, Trap dished out an oyster pie. It was baked in coconut oil and lard and covered with extra-hot chili powder.

After the meal, I dragged myself home.

At three o'clock in the morning, I woke up with a terrible stomachache. My belly was rumbling nonstop. I sounded just like the

Rodent's Express chugging into the train station.

Chug, chug . . . chuuuuuggg, chug, chug · · ·

I had never felt so sick in my life. I called the doctor. First he yelled at me for eating SHELLFISH. Then he yelled at me for eating FRIED FOOD. Then he yelled at me just to YELL at me. He said there wasn't much he could do for me. I needed to get a lot of rest.

I burst into tears. "But I'm supposed to leave on vacation tonight!" I cried. "I'm going to Egypt. I'm going to see the pyramids!"

The doctor snorted. "Leaving? Tonight?" he scoffed. "Not a chance! You'll be in bed for a couple of days at least!"

Crushed, I crawled under my covers.

Another trip gone sour, just like my tummy.

A REEKING RAT'S NEST

I spent the next few days in bed. My cousin, on the other paw, felt just fine. He called me from the airport to tell me he was headed off on his vacation. He was going to Club Mouse, a super-popular singles resort.

By this time, I felt pretty sorry for myself. So I called Ms. Sweetpaws. She listened to me in silence. Then she coughed. "Mr. Stilton, I'm afraid I only have **one place left**," she explained. "It's called the Ratty Tatty Hotel. Would you like to hear more?"

I told her I would. I really needed a vacation. Plus, how bad could it be?

I listened to her description with wide-open ears.

Ratty Tatty Hotel

Location: Catstinko, in the heart of Furball City

Daytime Activities: One mile to Rankrat Beach; swim at your own risk

Nightlife: Crickets, mosquitoes, and bloodsucking bats

Category: Half a cheese triangle

Price: $100 a day per rodent*

* Please note: The following luxuries must be purchased separately: electricity ($20); toilet paper ($5); running water ($20); room key ($15); courtesy from the staff, including greetings ($25); use of elevator to be booked 24 hours in advance ($25); use of stairs ($5); air ($30).

 **5 CHEESE TRIANGLES**
Magnificent, super-luxurious hotel

 **4 CHEESE TRIANGLES**
Charming, top-notch hotel

 **3 CHEESE TRIANGLES**
Comfortable hotel

 **2 CHEESE TRIANGLES**
Decent hotel

 **1 cheese triangle**
Simple guesthouse; in fact, very simple

 **1/2 CHEESE TRIANGLE**
Reeking rat's nest

When Ms. Sweetpaws finished reading, I could barely squeak. **Stale Swiss balls!** My vacation was turning into a total nightmare! "Oh, yes, I almost forgot one small detail . . ." Ms. Sweetpaws continued.

I giggled. Ms. Sweetpaws must be pulling my paw. Now she'd tell me all about the **fabumouse** resort she had *really* found. I couldn't wait to hear about the pool. And the beautiful sunsets. And the king-size bed. But she kept talking about the Ratty Tatty. "You'll have to share the room with another rodent," she explained. "She's very young and **very friendly**, though."

I blinked. It wasn't a joke? There really was a Ratty Tatty Hotel? Half a cheese triangle? A reeking rat's nest?

I was shocked. "I have to sh-sh-sh-share a r-r-room," I stuttered, "with a rodent I've n-n-never m-m-m-met?"

Ms. Sweetpaws scolded me. "Mr. Stilton, it's not my fault you've canceled 4 trips!" she squeaked. "This is what's left. Now, if you're interested, you leave tomorrow morning by bus. If not, I have a list of rodents who would love to go!"

I accepted. What could I do? It was the RATTY TATTY HOTEL or nothing. Yes, I'd just have to forget about the trips I'd missed out on. Forget the plush resorts. Forget the exciting sights. Forget the all-you-can-eat cheese danish at the pool bar. Sobbing, I packed my suitcase.

The next day, I scampered down to the bus station. I climbed aboard a rusty old bus called the DUMP EXPRESS.

You're Here, Too, Boss?

With a sigh, I sank into my seat. I was so tired. Maybe I could catch a few Z's on the ride to Catstinko. I stared out the window, eyes half closed. Then I saw her. Pink sneakers, pink backpack, pink headphones. Yes, it was that annoying assistant of mine, **Pinky Pick**! She had a huge suitcase on wheels covered in pink fake fur. Pinky was directing it from afar with a **REMOTE CONTROL**.

A few minutes later, she boarded the bus. The driver closed the doors. Then we took off. That's when Pinky started to sing.

"I KNOW A SONG THAT DRIVES MICE WILD,

Pinky was directing her suitcase from afar . . .

BUT I DON'T CARE
,CAUSE IT MAKES ME SMILE!
YEAH, YEAH, YEAH . . ."

she squeaked.

I heard the passengers begin to murmur.
Pinky's singing got louder and louder.

"I KNOW A SONG
THAT DRIVES MICE WILD,
BUT I DON'T CARE
,CAUSE IT MAKES ME SMILE!
YEAH, YEAH, YEAH . .
YEAH, YEAH, YEAH, YEAH

The other rodents began to stamp their paws.

"**Enough already!**" one mouse cried.

"*MAKE HER STOP!*" another insisted.

"KICK HER OFF THE BUS!" someone else suggested.

Pinky just kept on singing. I closed my eyes. Cheese niblets! I had the worst luck!

First the bad mussels. Then the Ratty Tatty Hotel. And now **Pinky Pick**. Maybe I needed to get myself a lucky charm or something. My great-uncle Beady had one. It was a teeny, tiny rubber mouse he had gotten from a cheeseball machine. He carried it with him everywhere he went. He lived to be 120!

Just then, I noticed something. It was quiet. **UH-OH**, I thought. I had a bad feeling in my stomach. Only one thing could make Pinky stop annoying the other passengers. I looked up. I was right. Pinky had spotted me. She stuck her snout right next to mine.

"**Boss! Boooss!** You're here, too???" she shrieked.

I cringed. Pinky didn't seem to notice. "So, Boss Mouse, where are you going?" she asked.

I told her I was headed for Catstinko.

"Me, too!" she exclaimed.

I chewed my whiskers. "I'm staying at the Ratty Tatty Hotel," I continued.

"Me, too!" Pinky shouted.

I twisted my tail into a knot. "I'm in room **13**," I finished.

"Me, too!" Pinky yelled.

I began to pull out all of my fur. Pinky grinned from ear to ear. "Let's shake paws, Boss!" she squeaked happily. "We're gonna be roomies!"

Then she winked. "Do you snore, Boss? Or sleepwalk? Hey, Boss, do you have athlete's paw? Do your paws stink?"

Before I could answer, Pinky went on. "And here's some more

GOOD NEWS, Boss Mouse. My entire Gerbil Scout troop will also sleep in room **13**! Isn't that great?" she giggled. "We'll camp on the floor with our tents and sleeping bags! It's going to be more fun than a barrel of clown mice! Isn't that cool, Boss?? **Booooooooooss???**"

I didn't answer.

I couldn't answer. I had fainted.

PEANUT BUTTER AND JUNE BUGS!

I came to with a start. Some mouse was waving a slice of cheese under my snout. I jumped up and raced to the front of the bus. "I want to get off!" I squeaked.

The driver just snorted. "Too late."

I looked out the window. An old wooden sign hung from a crooked lamppost. It read

Catstinko, Furball City

I closed my eyes. Maybe this was all just a bad dream.

I blinked. This wasn't just a bad dream. It was a **NIGHTMARE**! In front of me stood a run-down old house. The windows were broken. The curtains were torn. And the door was hanging off the hinges. Instead of a

In front of me stood a run-down old house.

swimming pool, there was a wooden tub. A rodent sat in the tub, waving his paws in the air. A cloud of $mosquitoes$ buzzed over his head.

A greasy-looking rat opened the door. "Welcome to the Ratty Tatty," he snickered. "The name's Freddy Fleafur, but my friends call me Itchy. You're just in time for lunch." He gave me a sandwich and a drink.

I was starving. I bit into the sandwich. Cheese niblets! It was awful. I tried to wash it down with the drink. But that was even worse.

"What is this?" I spluttered.

Freddy smirked. "Peanut butter and june bugs with moldy mozzarella milk," he said, chuckling.

I choked. "June bugs? Mold? I want to go home!" I squeaked.

Freddy "Itchy" Fleafur

Freddy chuckled again. "Sorry, Mousey," he snickered. "The bus won't be back until next **MONTH**. Just relax, put your paws up. Here, have something else to eat."

Before I could stop him, he shoved another disgusting sandwich into my mouth. This one was crunchy. I spat out a spider leg. Then something moved under the bread. A beetle crawled out over my tongue and headed up my nose.

"Aaaah!!!!!" I shrieked. "I want to go hooooooooooooooooooooooooooome!"

Just then, **Pinky Pick** wandered over. She was waving the special activity insert from her **Fur Kids Only** magazine.

"Follow me, Boss," she squeaked. "We're going to play some great games. I promise you'll have fun!"

I sighed. I began flipping through the magazine. They really did look like fun games.

Pinky Pick

GAMES TO PLAY ON VACATION

as suggested by... **Pinky Pick**

Young mice, take note! Always ask for your parents' permission before you start any of the games!

SUNSHINEY GAMES

Cloud Shapes

You'll need: a meadow, the sky.

Lie down on the grass (or on a blanket), on your back with your snout in the air. Look at the clouds and try to find the one with the most unusual shape: a bird, a plane, a mouse . . . or even a slice of cheese!

Searching for Buried Paws

This game is not as easy as it sounds.

You'll need: ideally, a sandy beach, but a bucket full of sand or flour will work.

Each player takes a turn sticking his paws under the sand, keeping them slightly apart. Then, paws still under the sand, he must try to make them touch. Don't be fooled! This game is not as easy as it sounds.

Catch That Shadow

You'll need: a meadow, lots of friends, a sunny day.

Divide into pairs. Each player must try to step on her teammates' shadows. The winner is the player whose shadow never gets stepped on!

The Mouse's Clock!

You'll need: lots of friends, a playground, a wall.

One of the players stands at the wall, facing it so she can't see the others. The rest of the players stand several feet behind her. The rodent near the wall shouts, "The mouse's clock goes ticktock!" As she's squeaking, all the others run toward her. The minute she's finished, she turns around. The others must freeze on the spot. If a player is caught moving or wobbling, he takes the place of the rodent at the wall. If no one is caught, then the mouse farthest away must go to the wall.

The game continues until one player touches the back of the player at the wall. He is the winner.

"The mouse's clock goes ticktock!"

The Twins Game

You'll need: lots of friends, an open space, a whistle.

Choose a mouse to be the referee and give him the whistle. The other players divide into pairs of "twins." Then everyone starts running around all over the place. Every time the referee blows the whistle, each pair must grab paws, sit down, and shout "Twins!" The last couple to come together is out of the game. The game continues until the last remaining pair is declared the winner.

The Burning-Hot Cheese Ball

You'll need: one ball, lots of friends.

Standing in a circle, the players pass the ball around. As they pass it, they sing:

"Pass the cheese, if you please.

Pass the cheese, if you please.

Do not drop it in a pot,

Pass the cheese, it's burning hot!"

At the end of the rhyme, the player left holding the ball is eliminated. The last remaining player is the winner!

The Frog
and the Shark

You'll need: one young mouse and one adult; the sea, a lake, or a swimming pool; a pair of inflatable water wings.

The young mouse puts on the inflatable water wings. She splashes into the water and shouts "Ribbit!" just like a frog. The adult dives in after the young mouse. He splashes after the frog, pretending he is a shark. Holey cheese! Watch those teeth!

I am the frog!

I am the shark!

You Make Me Stick!

You'll need: a big space and lots of friends.

One of the players pretends a part of his body (paw, ear, tail, etc.) has glue on it. He "sticks" this part onto another player. Now the two have to walk, run, sit down, and get up without coming unstuck! Any player who brushes against the first glued pair sticks to them, too. The more players who get glued on, the sillier it gets!

The Marble Meet

You'll need: some marbles, a sandy beach, a small shovel, and some water.

Trace a long, wide marble track on the beach, with lots of curves, some holes, and a few bumps. Put up some sand banks along the track's sides to keep the marbles inside. (You may want to ask an adult to help you dig.) Mark the start and finish lines. Now each player chooses a marble, and the race is on!

The Relay Race

You'll need: lots of players; two pawkerchiefs; a meadow, beach, or playground; and a big rock.

Place the rock on the ground. Then stand about fifty feet away from the rock. Divide the players into two teams with an even number of players on each team. Each team gives a pawkerchief to one of its members, who runs toward the rock, touches it, and runs back to the next player. The next player takes the pawkerchief and runs to the rock and back. The team that runs the fastest wins the game.

Keep Away Water Ball

You'll need: a soft ball, a lake or a pool, a lot of friends (the more the better!), and an adult mouse for a lifeguard.

Make a wide circle in the water with one player standing in the middle. The other players throw the ball to one another over the head of the middle player, who tries to catch the ball in midair. If she gets it, she can leave the middle of the circle, and the player who threw the ball takes her place. If the ball falls into the water, the one who threw it has to go in the middle.

The Rain Dance

You'll need: a shoe box, pebbles, clear tape, and colored markers.

Decorate the shoe box with the markers. Then write the words "rain box" on the outside. Place a pawful of pebbles inside the box. Put the lid on and seal it with tape.

Now begin to dance in a circle, shaking the rain box. Look up in the sky. Are those storm clouds up there? If not, keep those paws tapping!

A Hop, a Skip, and a Sack

You'll need: lots of players, lots of sacks, and a meadow or a beach.

Mark the race's start and finish lines. Each player gets into a sack and tries to hop or jump to the finish line. Whoever gets there first wins!

Book It!

You'll need: lots of players and lots of books.

Get ready to race! Mark the start and finish lines. Each player must run with a book between his knees. If the book drops, the player must go back to the starting line and begin again.

The Egg Race

You'll need: lots of players, lots of teaspoons, and lots of eggs.

Mark the race's start and finish lines. Each player takes one egg and one teaspoon. The eggs must be balanced inside the teaspoons — one for each rodent. Every mouse must run the race with the teaspoon in his paw. If the egg falls off, the player is disqualified.

RAINY DAY GAMES

Ghost Party!

You'll need: a room, some old sheets, a pair of scissors, and lots of friends.

Ask an adult to help you! Spread a bunch of sheets on the floor. On each sheet, cut out holes for two eyes and a mouth near the center of the sheet. When you're finished, drape the sheets over yourselves so that you can see out of the eyeholes. Wave your paws about and make some scary sounds. Now ask one of your friends to be a judge. Hold a contest to decide who makes the scariest ghost mouse. Say boo!

Booooooooooo! I am a ghost!

A Chain of Little Mice

You'll need: some long strips of white paper, a pair of scissors, and colored markers.

Ask an adult to help you! Fold the strip of paper several times so that it looks like an accordion. On the first fold, draw the outline of a mouse. Its paws must reach the edge of the paper on both sides. With the help of an adult, cut all around the drawing, leaving out the bits where the upper paws touch the paper's edges. Now unfold the paper and you'll have a chain of mice holding one another's paws. Color the paper chain and hang it on the wall.

1. Fold the paper strip.

2. Draw the outline on the first fold.

3. Cut along the outline, and you'll have a mouse chain.

Sock Theater

You'll need: some old socks, scraps of colored cloth, glue, a pair of scissors, and lots of friends.

Let's play together.

Ask an adult to help you! Take the colored cloth and draw on it a pair of eyes, a mouth, and some strips for the hair. Cut them out and glue them onto the socks, at the toe end. Now put your paw inside the sock and say hello to your new friend! Use a funny voice to make your sock puppet talk. You can even give it a funny name, like Smellypaw or Holeytoes. Gather all of your friends together and put on a sock puppet show.

Blind As a Mouse

You'll need: a blindfold, lots of friends.

Blindfold one of the players. Turn him slowly around and around at least ten times, then let him go. The player must try to catch one of the other players. Then he must guess which friend it is just by touching him. If he guesses correctly, the player who has been caught will take his place.

Doggie Makeover

You'll need: a few magazines, sheets of paper, a pair of scissors, and glue.

Ask an adult to help you! Cut out any pictures of dogs you find in the magazines. Then cut out the different dog parts (the tail, the ears, the head, the body, the legs). On a piece of paper, create a new kind of dog by gluing together the different body parts (the tail from one dog, the ears from another, etc.). Then make up a funny name for your new dog, like Cockerpoodle or Bulldoodle.

Name That Show!

You'll need: lots of friends, a timer or a watch with a second hand.

One of the players leaves the room. The rest of the players think of the name of a television show. When the player comes back, the others try to act out the name. The player can ask questions, but the others can only answer yes or no. When the player finally guesses correctly, another player takes her place. The one who takes the least amount of time to guess the right show wins!

The Secret Code

You'll need: pencil and paper.

Cheese niblets! It's fun to write in secret code. Here's
an example of a very secret code you can use with your
best friend. Each letter has been replaced by a number.

A = 1	H = 8	O = 15	V = 22
B = 2	I = 9	P = 16	W = 23
C = 3	J = 10	Q = 17	X = 24
D = 4	K = 11	R = 18	Y = 25
E = 5	L = 12	S = 19	Z = 26
F = 6	M = 13	T = 20	
G = 7	N = 14	U = 21	

For example: "Hello, I am Geronimo" becomes

8 5 12 12 15,   9   1 13   7 5 18 15 14 9 13 15

Here's another code: Replace each letter with the
following one, like this.

A = B	H = I	O = P	V = W
B = C	I = J	P = Q	W = X
C = D	J = K	Q = R	X = Y
D = E	K = L	R = S	Y = Z
E = F	L = M	S = T	Z = A
F = G	M = N	T = U	
G = H	N = O	U = V	

For example: "Hello, I am Geronimo" becomes

IFMMP, J BN HFSPOJNP

Here's another, more complicated code. Each letter has a corresponding symbol.

A = +	H = @	O = <	V = ^
B = −	I = #	P = ∞	W = /
C = x	J = "	Q = Σ	X = ç
D = :	K = (	R = ~	Y = £
E = &	L = '	S = =	Z = >
F = *	M =)	T = §	
G = $	N = °	U = %	

For example: "Hello, I am Geronimo" becomes

@&''<, # +) $&~<°#)<

Invent your own personal code! Remember, any code can work as long as it follows a pattern.

A =	H =	O =	V =
B =	I =	P =	W =
C =	J =	Q =	X =
D =	K =	R =	Y =
E =	L =	S =	Z =
F =	M =	T =	
G =	N =	U =	

Invent
your own
personal
code!

Can You Squeak It?

You'll need: lots of friends, pencil, and paper.

Have you ever met a mouse from another country? Did he squeak a different language? It's fun to learn new languages. Here are just a few words and phrases you can learn in another language. For example, "Hello!" in French is "Bonjour!"

HELLO!
HOW ARE YOU?
HOW OLD ARE YOU?
WHERE ARE YOU FROM?
YES! NO!
PLEASE . . .
THANK YOU!

In Italian it's Buon Giorno!

In French Hello is Bonjour!

JAMBO!   GUTEN MORGEN!   KONNICHIWA!   ¡HOLA!

SWAHILI   GERMAN   JAPANESE   SPANISH

Get Well, Dolly!

You'll need: your favorite doll, toilet paper, tape, and a piece of paper.

Pretend that one of your dolls is sick. Then open up your own doll hospital! Check your doll from head to toe. Touch her forehead to see if she is feverish. Tap her knee to check her reflexes. Tell her to say "Aah!" Then make a bandage for your doll using the toilet paper and tape, or write a prescription for the doll's medicine on a piece of paper.

STRASVICE! SHALOM! SAVUBONA! SALAAM! ZAOSCIANHAO!

RUSSIAN   HEBREW   ZULU   ARABIC   CHINESE

Crazyhopper!

You'll need: an empty room, some friends, a radio.

Turn on some fun music. Then line up in single file. Place your paws on the shoulders of the friend standing in front of you. Hop forward together on your right paw. Do it again on your left. Then hop backward, then forward. If you're all still standing, start all over again. Keep hopping faster and faster to the music's beat. Watch those tails!

Don't Leaf Me Hanging!

You'll need: lots of leaves, a heavy book, a sketchbook or pad of paper, some glue, markers, and a book on plants.

Pick up lots of different leaves. Identify them in the plant book. Then press them between the pages of a heavy book. When they have dried out — it might take a few days — glue them into your sketchbook. Underneath each leaf, write the name of the tree to which it belongs.

Hum That Tune!

You'll need: lots of friends, a watch with a second hand.

Divide into two teams, plus a singer. The singer hums a well-known song. Each team has one minute to guess the name of the song. The team that guesses the most song names in half an hour wins the game.

One Potato, Two Potato, Three Potato, STAMP!

You'll need: some raw potatoes, a small knife, a stamp pad, sheets of paper.

Ask an adult to help you! Cut the potato in half and on the flat side carve out a simple design (a heart, a flower, a star, a slice of cheese).

Press the potato into the stamp pad. Then press it onto the paper. Congratulations! You are now an official potato stamper!

The Tree of Me

You'll need: a big piece of white cardboard, some colored markers, and as many family photographs as you can get your paws on. (Make sure it's OK with your mom and dad before you begin.)

Using the markers, copy the tree on this page onto your white board. Make it as big as possible. Then write the names of all your family members inside the yellow spaces — your own name, your father's, your mother's, your grandparents', your great-grandparents', your aunts' and uncles', your cousins', etc. If you have a big enough space, you can also write their dates and places of birth. Then add the photographs. How many branches are on your tree?

Picture-Perfect Pebbles

You'll need: lots of round stones gathered on the banks of rivers or streams or at the ocean, an acrylic paint set, and a pencil.

Ask an adult to help you! Wash the stones well with soap and water. Make a pencil drawing of your favorite animal (a mouse is always nice!) on the dry stone. Then paint over your drawing with the colored acrylic paints. You can use the stones as paperweights or start your own pawmade stone collection.

Framed by a Shell

You'll need: lots of seashells, a piece of cardboard, some all-purpose glue, and markers.

Gather lots of different shells. Make sure that they are all empty. Then wash them with soap and water. Dry them off, then glue them along the cardboard's edge to create a special frame. Glue a photograph of your favorite sea creature inside the frame.

Chatterbox Challenge

You'll need: lots of friends, a watch with a second hand.

One player will be the referee. He chooses a topic such as sports, school, movies, or even cheese. The players take their turns squeaking about the topic for sixty seconds. They can say whatever they like, without pausing for too long and always sticking to the topic. At the end, there's a vote: The most interesting or the funniest of the squeakers is the winner!

Make Your Own Magazine

You'll need: several sheets of paper, a camera.

Make your own fun vacation magazine! First you'll need to take lots of pictures of your trip. If you're at the beach, take photographs of seashells, jellyfish, crabs, and, of course, your friends and family.

At the lake, look for tadpoles, fish, and crickets. Take pictures of your tent or cabin. Don't forget to say cheese!

Once you've developed the pictures, paste them down on your paper. Write a caption under each picture. Now make photocopies of each page. Then staple the pages together. Clap your paws together. You just made your own magazine!

Great! A crab pinched my finger. Now I will have something to write about in my magazine.

The Vacation Superposter

You'll need: a large sheet of colored poster board.

Collect all of your travel tickets such as airplane, bus, or railroad receipts. Pick up postcards or brochures from the places you visit on your vacation. Gather together leaves, flowers, or seashells you may find. If you go to the beach, put some sand in a plastic bag. If you go to the mountains, pick up a small rock.

Now glue the postcards on your posterboard. Paste the things you have collected around the postcards. Then write a description of each object. For example, "Pine needles from Furry Tail Forest" or "White sand from Slippery Paws Resort."

Hang your poster in your room. Whenever you need a break, just look at your poster. Surprise! Instant vacation!

I COULD BUY
EARPLUGS . . .

I was still flipping through the games in **Fur Kids Only** when Pinky started squeaking. "Let's go play marbles, everyone! Come on, Boss. We'll have fun!"

I groaned. RANCID RAT HAIRS! I just wasn't in the mood for Pinky's fun and games. I was on vacation, after all. I just wanted to be by myself. To enjoy the natural wildlife. I looked around. The only wildlife I saw was a swarm of mosquitoes and two sick-looking garden slugs.

Well, maybe I could play one or two of Pinky's games, I decided. Before I knew it, I was rolling marbles down a huge sand track. Then I ran in an egg race, made a sock puppet, and even danced the rain dance.

I must admit, Pinky was right. I did have fun. Loads of fun. In fact, I think it is safe to say that I had more fun than a day at the Swiss Cheese Festival.

At dinner, I had another surprise. It turned out Freddy Fleafur was actually an excellent cook. Once we told him we didn't like bugs, he came up with a whole new menu. We had FRESH-SQUEEZED LEMONADE, BLUE CHEESE PIE, MELTED CHEDDAR ROLLS, AND FRESH STRAWBERRY CHEESECAKE FOR DESSERT. It was all so yummy, I chowed down 3 helpings!

Soon it was time for bed. I wasn't looking forward to sleeping in the same room with Pinky and her friends. They'd probably be up giggling away half the night. But I was a grown mouse. I needed my rest.

Of course, in the end, I was right. Pinky and her friends did end up squeaking and telling silly stories all night long. But I was the mouse laughing the loudest! Yes, I'm embarrassed to say, I had the best time.

The days seemed to fly by. Before I knew it, it was the day before we left for home.

I climbed into the bathtub for a relaxing soak. Pinky really wasn't such a bad mouse, I decided. In fact, Pinky could be a lot of fun. *Maybe next year I'd go on vacation with Pinky again,* I thought. I sank deeper into the tub and closed my eyes.

Just then, I heard someone singing in a loud, obnoxious voice outside the bathroom.

"I KNOW A SONG THAT DRIVES MICE WILD, BUT I DON'T CARE 'CAUSE IT MAKES ME SMILE! YEAH, YEAH, YEAH . . ."

I knew who was squeaking. I already

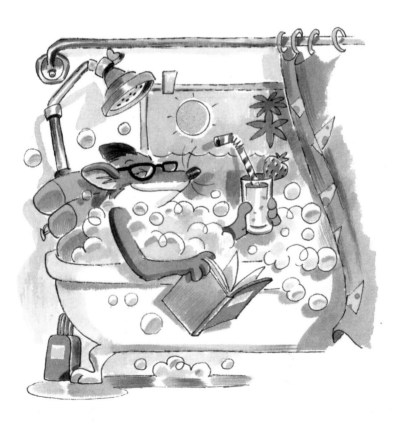

knew that irritating song. I already knew that horrible, ear-piercing squeak.

I sighed. I guess I wasn't *really* ready for another vacation with Pinky Pick. Then again, I could always buy earplugs. . . .

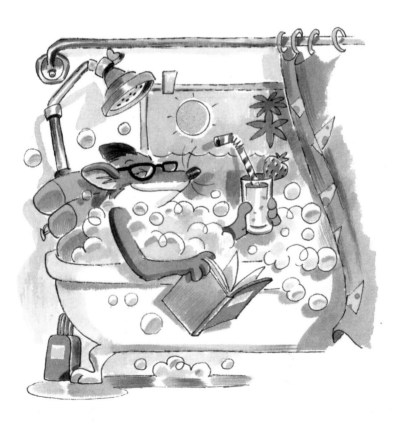

ABOUT THE AUTHOR

Born in New Mouse City, Mouse Island, Geronimo Stilton is Rattus Emeritus of Mousomorphic Literature and of Neo-Ratonic Comparative Philosophy. For the past twenty years, he has been running *The Rodent's Gazette*, New Mouse City's most widely read daily newspaper.

Stilton was awarded the Ratitzer Prize for his scoop on *The Curse of the Cheese Pyramid*. He has also received the Andersen 2000 Prize for Personality of the Year. One of his bestsellers won the 2002 eBook Award for world's best ratlings' electronic book. His works have been published all over the globe.

In his spare time, Mr. Stilton collects antique cheese rinds and plays golf. But what he most enjoys is telling stories to his nephew Benjamin.

Don't miss any of my other fabumouse adventures!

#1 Lost Treasure of the Emerald Eye

#2 The Curse of the Cheese Pyramid

#3 Cat and Mouse in a Haunted House

#4 I'm Too Fond of My Fur!

#5 Four Mice Deep in the Jungle

#6 Paws Off, Cheddarface!

#7 Red Pizzas for a Blue Count

#8 Attack of the Bandit Cats

and coming soon

#10 All Because of a Cup of Coffee

Want to read my next adventure?
It's sure to be a fur-raising experience!

ALL BECAUSE OF A CUP OF COFFEE

I, Geronimo Stilton, was in love! At the coffee shop one morning, I spotted the most beautiful rodent in the world. Unfortunately, I immediately tripped and ended up with my tail in a toaster. I was one mortified mouse! But I was still determined to prove my love. So I joined my family on a journey to the Eighth Wonder of the World! There I made a discovery so amazing, I knew it would help me win the heart of my darling ratlette....

THE RODENT'S GAZETTE

1. **Main Entrance**
2. **Printing presses (where the books and newspaper are printed)**
3. **Accounts department**
4. **Editorial room (where the editors, illustrators, and designers work)**
5. **Geronimo Stilton's office**
6. **Storage space for Geronimo's books**

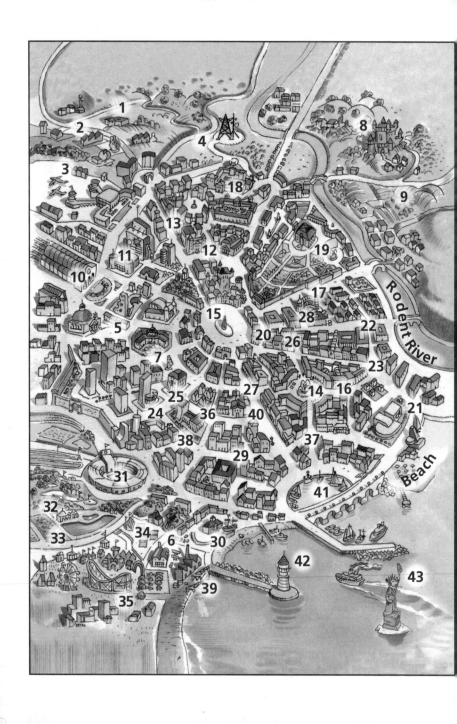

Map of New Mouse City

1. Industrial Zone
2. Cheese Factories
3. Angorat International Airport
4. WRAT Radio and Television Station
5. Cheese Market
6. Fish Market
7. Town Hall
8. Snotnose Castle
9. The Seven Hills of Mouse Island
10. Mouse Central Station
11. Trade Center
12. Movie Theater
13. Gym
14. Catnegie Hall
15. Singing Stone Plaza
16. The Gouda Theater
17. Grand Hotel
18. Mouse General Hospital
19. Botanical Gardens
20. Cheap Junk for Less (Trap's store)
21. Parking Lot
22. Mouseum of Modern Art
23. University and Library
24. *The Daily Rat*
25. *The Rodent's Gazette*
26. Trap's House
27. Fashion District
28. The Mouse House Restaurant
29. Environmental Protection Center
30. Harbor Office
31. Mousidon Square Garden
32. Golf Course
33. Swimming Pool
34. Blushing Meadow Tennis Courts
35. Curlyfur Island Amusement Park
36. Geronimo's House
37. New Mouse City Historic District
38. Public Library
39. Shipyard
40. Thea's House
41. New Mouse Harbor
42. Luna Lighthouse
43. The Statue of Liberty

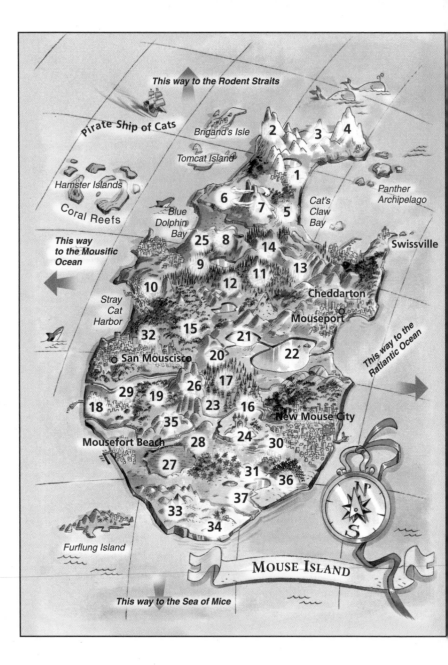

Map of Mouse Island

1. Big Ice Lake
2. Frozen Fur Peak
3. Slipperyslopes Glacier
4. Coldcreeps Peak
5. Ratzikistan
6. Transratania
7. Mount Vamp
8. Roastedrat Volcano
9. Brimstone Lake
10. Poopedcat Pass
11. Stinko Peak
12. Dark Forest
13. Vain Vampires Valley
14. Goose Bumps Gorge
15. The Shadow Line Pass
16. Penny Pincher Lodge
17. Nature Reserve Park
18. Las Ratayas Marinas
19. Fossil Forest
20. Lake Lake

21. Lake Lake Lake
22. Lake Lakelakelake
23. Cheddar Crag
24. Cannycat Castle
25. Valley of the Giant Sequoia
26. Cheddar Springs
27. Sulfurous Swamp
28. Old Reliable Geyser
29. Vole Vail
30. Ravingrat Ravine
31. Gnat Marshes
32. Munster Highlands
33. Mousehara Desert
34. Oasis of the Sweaty Camel
35. Cabbagehead Hill
36. Rattytrap Jungle
37. Rio Mosquito

Dear mouse friends,
Thanks for reading, and farewell
till the next book.
It'll be another whisker-licking-good
adventure, and that's a promise!

Geronimo Stilton